A NOTE TO PARENTS

When your children are ready to "step into reading," giving them the right books is as crucial to their development as giving them the right food to eat. **Step into Reading®** books feature exciting stories and information reinforced with lively, colorful illustrations that make learning to read fun, satisfying, and rewarding. We have even taken *extra* steps to keep your child engaged by offering Step into Reading Sticker books, Step into Reading Math books, and Step into Reading Phonics books, in addition to fabulous fiction and nonfiction.

Learning to read, Step by Step:

- **Super Early** books (Preschool–Kindergarten) support pre-reading skills. Parent and child can engage in "see and say" reading using the strong picture cues and the few simple words on each page.
- **Early** books (Preschool–Kindergarten) let emergent readers tackle one or two short sentences of large type per page.
- **Step 1** books (Preschool–Grade 1) have the same easy-to-read type as Early, but with more words per page.
- **Step 2** books (Grades 1–3) offer longer and slightly more difficult text while introducing contractions and clauses. Children are often drawn to our exciting natural science nonfiction titles at this level.
- **Step 3** books (Grades 2–3) present paragraphs, chapters, and fully developed plot lines in fiction and nonfiction.
- **Step 4** books (Grades 2–4) feature thrilling nonfiction illustrated with exciting photographs for independent as well as reluctant readers.

Remember: The grade levels assigned to the six steps are intended only as guides. Some children move through all six steps rapidly; others climb the steps over a period of a few years. Either way, these books will help children "step into reading" for life!

For Raymond's aunts:
Katherine, Lucy, Stephanie, Uma, and Lori
—V.M.N.

For Cheryl—D.A.

Text copyright © 2002 by Vaunda Micheaux Nelson.
Illustrations copyright © 2002 by Derek Anderson.
All rights reserved under International and Pan-American Copyright Conventions.
Published in the United States by Random House, Inc., New York, and simultaneously in
Canada by Random House of Canada Limited, Toronto.

www.randomhouse.com/kids

Library of Congress Cataloging-in-Publication Data
Nelson, Vaunda Micheaux. Ready? Set. Raymond! / by Vaunda Nelson ;
illustrated by Derek Anderson.
p. cm. — (Step into reading. Step 1 book) Contents: Slow down, Raymond — Raymond and
Roxy — New sneakers.
SUMMARY: Three stories in which a little boy does everything fast, from brushing his teeth
to making new friends to running races.
ISBN 0-375-81363-2 (trade) — ISBN 0-375-91363-7 (lib. bdg.)
[1. Speed—Fiction.] I. Anderson, Derek, ill. II. Title.
PZ7.N43773 Re 2002 [E]—dc21 2001041875

Printed in the United States of America First Edition June 2002 10 9 8 7 6 5 4 3 2 1

Step into Reading®

Ready? Set. Raymond!

by Vaunda Micheaux Nelson

illustrated by Derek Anderson

A Step 1 Book

Random House 🏠 New York

Slow Down, Raymond

Raymond does
things fast.

He brushes his teeth fast.

He eats breakfast fast.

"Slow down, Raymond.
Chew your food,"
Mama says.

Raymond slows down—
but not for long!

Raymond
dresses fast.

He kisses
Mama fast.

He runs
to school
fast.

"Slow down, Raymond.
Look both ways,"
the policeman says.

Raymond slows down—
but not for long!

He reads fast.

He counts fast.

He draws

pictures fast.

"Slow down, Raymond. There's no rush," his teacher says.

Raymond slows down— but not for long!

He runs
home fast.

He eats
dinner fast.

He brushes his
teeth fast.

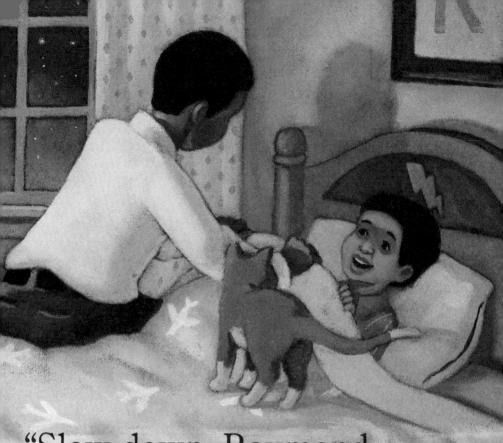

"Slow down, Raymond.
Time for bed," Papa says.

Raymond slowly closes his
eyes and . . .

… falls <u>fast</u> asleep!

Raymond and Roxy

Raymond sees
a new girl next door.
He wants a friend.

"Making friends
takes time,"
Mama says.

But Raymond cannot wait.

He runs next door.

"I'm Raymond!" he says.

The girl runs inside.

Raymond <u>walks</u> home.

"Making friends
takes time,"
Papa says.

But Raymond cannot wait.

He runs to the cookie jar.

He runs next door.

Raymond gives the girl
a cookie.

She takes a bite.

She smiles with cookie
in her teeth.

"I'm Roxy," she says.

Raymond and Roxy

become <u>fast</u> friends.

New Sneakers

Raymond likes to run.

He is going to be

in a big race.

He runs in the house,

in the yard,

at the park.

Raymond runs so much

he wears his sneakers out!
Mama buys Raymond
brand-new sneakers
for the big race.
They are white,
like clean sheets.

Raymond wants
his sneakers
to stay clean.
So he walks slowly
in the house,

in the yard,

to the park.

The race is starting.

"Ready?"

Raymond looks

at the dusty track.

"Set."

Raymond looks at
his clean new sneakers.

"Go!"

"Run, Raymond, run!"

Roxy shouts.

Raymond runs.

His sneakers get dirty.

But he wins the race!